Reach
for the Stars

and Other Advice
for Life's Journey

by Serge Bloch

STERLING

New York / London

For Meredith.
—S.B.

STERLING CHILDREN'S BOOKS
New York

An Imprint of Sterling Publishing
387 Park Avenue South
New York, NY 10016

STERLING CHILDREN'S BOOKS and the distinctive Sterling Children's Books logo are trademarks of Sterling Publishing Co., Inc.

Text © 2010 by Sterling Publishing Co., Inc.
Illustrations © 2010 by Serge Bloch

The artwork for this book was created using pen and ink drawings with photography.

Designed by Chrissy Kwasnik

ISBN 978-1-4027-7129-3

Library of Congress Cataloging-in-Publication Data
Bloch, Serge.
  Reach for the stars : and other advice for life's journey / by Serge Bloch.
     p. cm.
  Summary: A boy receives many confusing words of advice in the form of phrases like,
"Dust yourself off and get back in the saddle."
    ISBN 978-1-4027-7129-3 (hardcover-trade cloth : alk. paper) [1. Figures of speech--Fiction.
2. Humorous stories.] I. Title.
  PZ7.B61943Re 2010
  [E]--dc22
                              2009019721

Distributed in Canada by Sterling Publishing
c/o Canadian Manda Group, 165 Dufferin Street
Toronto, Ontario, Canada M6K 3H6
Distributed in the United Kingdom by GMC Distribution Services,
Castle Place, 166 High Street, Lewes, East Sussex, England BN7 1XU
For information about custom editions, special sales, and premium and corporate purchases,
please contact Sterling Special Sales at 800-805-5489 or specialsales@sterlingpublishing.com.

Printed in China
Lot #:
10 9 8
07/15

www.sterlingpublishing.com/kids

Y̲ou've got your whole life ahead of you!

Sometimes it'll be smooth sailing,

but other times it'll be a bumpy ride, with many forks in the road.

You might feel like a fish out of water

or like a small fish in a big pond.

That's your chance to make a splash!

If you sink like a stone, feeling like you're in over your head,

it may seem like you're fighting an uphill battle.

What better time to reach for the moon and shoot for the stars?

You won't always be top dog.

In fact, sometimes you'll be in the doghouse.

Dust yourself off! Get back in the saddle!

If you keep a cool head, and use some elbow grease . . .

. . . you can blaze your own trail

and march to the beat of a different drummer.

Always keep your eyes on the prize

and you might just hit the jackpot once in a while!

If not, there's always time to start from scratch

and turn the page on the past.

It's okay to have a change of heart

and it's only natural to make mountains out of molehills once in a while.

You may still be on pins and needles sometimes.

And the grass will seem greener on the other side.

But your friends will bend over backward to help you.

And soon you'll be rolling in clover!

When you have all your ducks in a row,

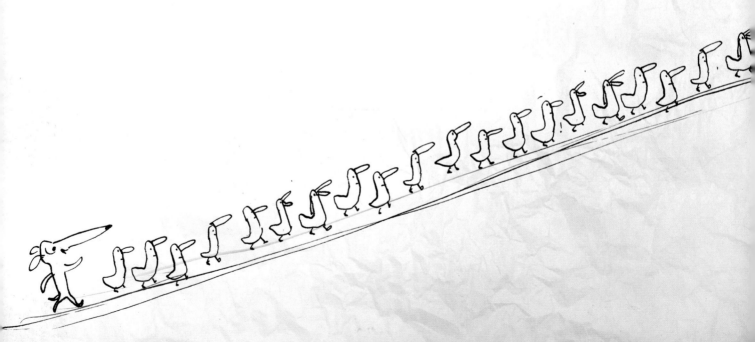

. . . you'll spread your wings and fly!